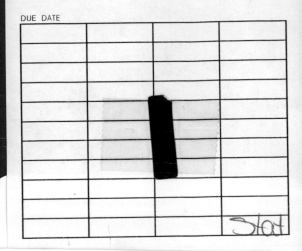

J
E

MAY   1992

Moss, Marissa

Knick knack pad-
dywack

DUE DATE

			Stat

KNICK KNACK
PADDYWACK

Marissa Moss

Houghton Mifflin Company
Boston 1992

For Larry and Livia, give a doggy bone

Library of Congress Cataloging-in-Publication Data

Moss, Marissa.
   Knick knack paddywack / Marissa Moss.
     p.   cm.
   Summary: In this variation and extension of the traditional counting song, "this old man" ends up blasting off and flying to the moon.
   ISBN 0-395-54701-6
   1. Folk songs, English — Texts. [1. Folk songs. 2. Counting.]
I. Title.
PZ8.3.M8466Kn   1992   91-17082
[E] — dc20   CIP
                       AC

Printed in the United States of America
WOZ 10 9 8 7 6 5 4 3 2 1

KNICK KNACK PADDYWACK

4

This old man, he played One.
He played knick knack, thump a thumb.
With a knick knack paddywack, give a dog a bone,
This old man went rolling home.

This old man, he played Two.
He played bip bop, tap a shoe.
With a bip bop hobblepop, give a dog a bone,
This old man went rolling home.

This old man, he played Three.
He played bim bum, bump a knee.
With a bim bum bumpabum, give a dog a bone,
This old man went rolling home.

This old man, he played Four.
He played jig jug, jump some more.
With a jig jug jugglebug, give a dog a bone,
This old man went rolling home.

This old man, he played Five.
He played tip tap, TV live.
With a tip tap bunnyrap, give a dog a bone,
This old man went rolling home.

This old man, he played Six.
He played click clack, kick some kicks.
With a click clack pattysmack, give a dog a bone,
This old man went rolling home.

7

This old man, he played Seven.
He played slip slap whap and then
With a slip slap rattatap, give a dog a bone,
This old man went rolling home.

This old man, he played Eight.
He played flip flop till quite late.
With a flip flop hippyhop, give a dog a bone,
This old man went rolling home.

This old man, he played Nine.
He played kick kwick, rain or shine.
With a kick kwick fiddlestick, give a dog a bone,
This old man went rolling home.

This old man, he played Ten.
He played splish splash, falling when,
With a splish splash crazycrash, give a dog a bone,
This old man went rolling home.

This old man, he played all.
He played each part, big and small.

With a brush bang hammerclang, give a dog a bone,
This old man went rolling home.

This old man, he counts Ten,
Nine, eight, seven, six, five, and then

Four, three, two, one!
Now blast off!
This old man goes soaring off.

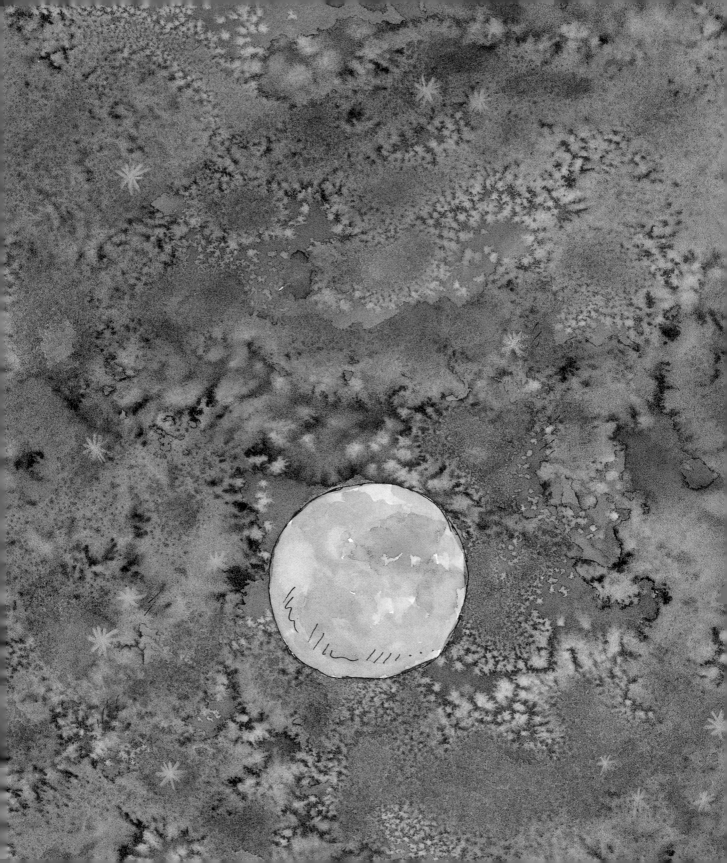

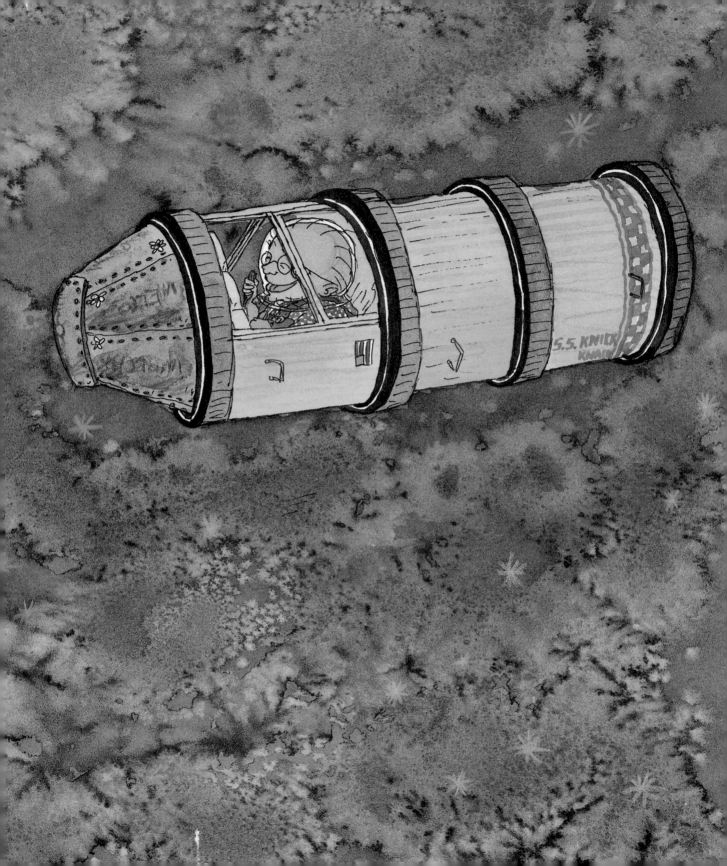

This old man, he flies high.
He plays knick knack in the sky.
With a knick knack paddywack, sing a dog a tune,
This old man's now on the moon.